Stone Soup

Retold by Lesley Sims

Illustrated by Georgien Overwater

Reading Consultant: Alison Kelly
Roehampton University

Once, there was a
poor man.

He came to
a cottage.

Knock!
Knock!

An old woman opened
the door.

"I can make soup from a stone," said the man.

"You can?" said the woman. "Show me."

She put a big pot of water on the fire.

8

The old man added a
shiny stone.

The soup bubbled.
The old man tasted it.

"An onion would make it better," he said.

11

So the old woman
chopped an onion

and popped it in.

The soup bubbled.
The old man tasted it.

"A potato would make it better," he said.

15

So the old woman
chopped a potato

and popped it in.

The soup bubbled.
The old man tasted it.

He licked his lips.
"Some meat would
make it better still."

So the old woman chopped some meat and popped it in.

21

The old man put it
into bowls.

"It *is* yummy," said
the old woman. "That
stone must be magic."

23

The old man smiled.

He washed the stone
and put it in his pocket.

"Stay for supper," said the woman. "We can have soup."

PUZZLES

Puzzle 1

Put these pictures in order.

A   B   C

D   E   F

Puzzle 2
Spot the six differences between these two pictures.

Puzzle 3

Find the things in the picture.

spoons   dog   flowers   table
bowls   bread   cat

Puzzle 4
Choose the right words for the pictures.

Yummy!   Oof!

Go away!

A
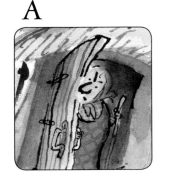

B

C

Answers to puzzles

Puzzle 1

C

B

D

F

E

A

Puzzle 2

Puzzle 3

spoon flowers

spoon

bowl

bowl

bread

table

cat

bowl dog bowl

Puzzle 4

A

Go away!

B

Yummy!

C

Oof!

About Stone Soup

This story is based on an old folktale from Europe. In some countries, it is called Nail Soup and a nail is used instead of a stone.

Designed by Michelle Lawrence
Series designer: Russell Punter

First published in 2009 by Usborne Publishing Ltd., Usborne House, 83-85 Saffron Hill, London EC1N 8RT, England. www.usborne.com
Copyright © 2009 Usborne Publishing Ltd.